HOPSCOTCH TWISTY TALES

Jack
and the
Bean Pie

by Laura North and Mike Phillips

W

This story is based on the traditional fairy tale, Jack and the Beanstalk, but with a new twist. You can read the original story in Hopscotch Fairy Tales. Can you make up a new twist of your own?

First published in 2010 by
Franklin Watts
338 Euston Road
London
NW1 3BH

Franklin Watts Australia
Level 17/207 Kent Street
Sydney
NSW 2000

Text © Laura North 2010
Illustrations © Mike Phillips 2010

The rights of Laura North to be identified as the author
and Mike Phillips as the illustrator of this Work have been asserted
in accordance with the Copyright, Designs and Patents Act, 1988.

A CIP catalogue record for this book is available
from the British Library.

ISBN 978 1 4451 0176 7 (hbk)
ISBN 978 1 4451 0182 8 (pbk)

Series Editor: Melanie Palmer
Series Advisor: Catherine Glavina
Series Designer: Peter Scoulding

Printed in China

Franklin Watts is a division of
Hachette Children's Books,
an Hachette UK company
www.hachette.co.uk

For Christian – L.N.

Once, a boy called Jack lived in
a tiny house with his mother.

They had no money and just
ate vegetables from their garden.
But Jack was very good at cooking.
He made delicious bean pies.

One day, he took the pies to the market to sell.

Bean Pies for Sale

"I'll buy your pies," said
an old man. "But I can only
pay with these magic beans."
Jack agreed and raced home.

Jack's mother was furious. "We need gold coins, not these useless beans!" she shouted.

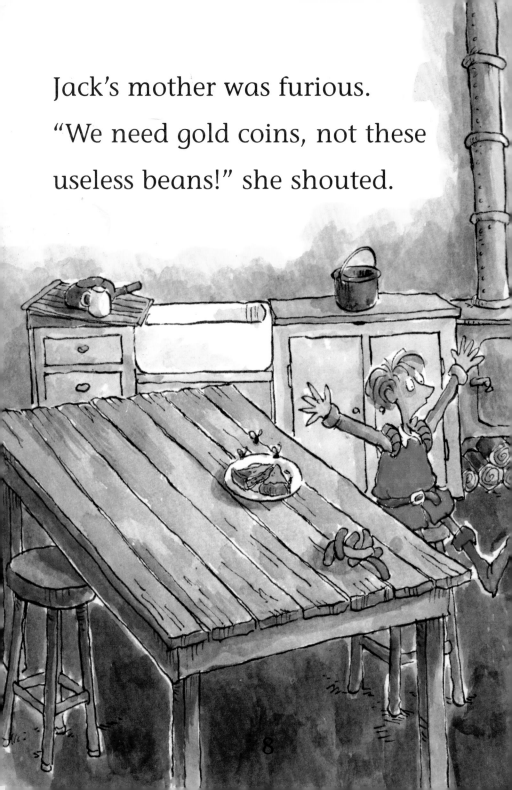

She grabbed some beans and threw them out of the window in anger.

The next day, there was a huge beanstalk in the garden. The beans were magic after all!

"I wonder what's at the top?"
thought Jack. He started to climb,
up and up, into the clouds, until ...

… he found another world!
There were enormous flowers,
the size of trees. He saw a bee
the size of a horse!

13

Then a voice boomed,

"Fe fi fo fum ..."

"What's that?" thought Jack.

The voice got louder.

"Fe fi fo fum,
I smell the blood
of an Englishman!"

Suddenly, a huge hairy giant stood in front of Jack.

He picked up Jack in one hand.

"Got you!" the giant growled.

Jack was terrified!

Jack had a few magic beans left in his pocket. He threw them at the giant and hoped they were still magic.

"Yum!" said the giant, "I love beans! They taste much better than humans."

19

Then the giant started to cry.

"I don't want to eat you at all,"
he sobbed. Big tears fell on Jack.
"The other giants make me
eat people. What can I do?"

Jack felt sorry for the giant.

"I've got an idea," he said.

"I can cook great pies. Let's tell the other giants they are human pies, but really fill them with beans!"

"Come and get your human pies!" shouted Jack.

The hungry giants soon arrived.

25

As the giants gobbled up the pies,
Jack bravely jumped up.
"SURPRISE! The pies are full of
beans, not people!" he said.

"But this is the best pie I've ever had!" roared one giant.

"More bean pies!" they shouted.

The pies were so tasty that the giants forgot about eating people.

Soon Jack became rich and famous from his bean pies. The giants never tried to eat humans again.

Puzzle 1

Put these pictures in the correct order.
Which event do you think is most important?
Now try making up your own ending!

Puzzle 2

1. I'd like to buy your pies.

2. I have a very strong sense of smell.

3. I love cooking!

4. I wonder if the beans are magic?

5. I don't have any coins.

6. I don't like the taste of humans.

Choose the correct speech bubbles for each character. Can you think of any others? Turn over to find the answers.

Answers

Puzzle 1

The correct order is: 1e, 2f, 3a, 4b, 5d, 6c

Puzzle 2

Jack: 3, 4

The giant: 2, 6

The old man: 1, 5

Look out for more Hopscotch Twisty Tales and Fairy Tales:

TWISTY TALES

The Three Little Pigs
and the New Neighbour
ISBN 978 1 4451 0175 0*
ISBN 978 1 4451 0181 1

Jack and the Bean Pie
ISBN 978 1 4451 0176 7*
ISBN 978 1 4451 0182 8

Brownilocks and the Three
Bowls of Cornflakes
ISBN 978 1 4451 0177 4 *
ISBN 978 1 4451 0183 5

Cinderella's Big Foot
ISBN 978 1 4451 0178 1*
ISBN 978 1 4451 0184 2

Little Bad Riding Hood
ISBN 978 1 4451 0179 8*
ISBN 978 1 4451 0185 9

Sleeping Beauty –
100 Years Later
ISBN 978 1 4451 0180 4*
ISBN 978 1 4451 0186 6

FAIRY TALES

The Three Little Pigs
ISBN 978 0 7496 7905 7

Little Red Riding Hood
ISBN 978 0 7496 7901 9*
ISBN 978 0 7496 7907 1

Goldilocks and the Three Bears
ISBN 978 0 7496 7903 3

Hansel and Gretel
ISBN 978 0 7496 7904 0

Rapunzel
ISBN 978 0 7496 7900 2*
ISBN 978 0 7496 7906 4

Rumpelstiltskin
ISBN 978 0 7496 7902 6*
ISBN 978 0 7496 7908 8

The Elves and the Shoemaker
ISBN 978 0 7496 8543 0

The Ugly Duckling
ISBN 978 0 7496 8538 6*
ISBN 978 0 7496 8544 7

Sleeping Beauty
ISBN 978 0 7496 8545 4

The Frog Prince
ISBN 978 0 7496 8540 9 *
ISBN 978 0 7496 8546 1

The Princess and
the Pea
ISBN 978 0 7496 8541 6*
ISBN 978 0 7496 8547 8

Dick Whittington
ISBN 978 0 7496 8542 3 *
ISBN 978 0 7496 8548 5

Cinderella
ISBN 978 0 7496 7417 5

Snow White and the Seven
Dwarfs
ISBN 978 0 7496 7418 2

The Pied Piper
of Hamelin
ISBN 978 0 7496 7419 9

Jack and the Beanstalk
ISBN 978 0 7496 7422 9

The Three Billy Goats Gruff
ISBN 978 0 7496 7420 5

The Emperor's New Clothes
ISBN 978 0 7496 7421 2